I hope you like my book

Callie

ENJOY!

Glitter
The Unicorn

By Callie Chapman

Illustrated By Bronwyne Carr Chapman

Author: Callie Chapman
Illustrator: Bronwyne Chapman
Printer: www.artbookbindery.com
Photo of Callie: Catherine Mayo

ISBN 978-0-9973968-0-5 (Hardback)
ISBN 978-0-9973968-1-2 (Paperback)

Printed and bound in Canada

Glitter
The Unicorn
By Callie Chapman

Six-year-old Callie lives in Alabama with her family. This imaginative, smart, and funny girl came up with the story of Glitter the Unicorn and her best friend Ellie, named after her favorite stuffed animals. Callie wanted to share her story with everyone, so she painted lots of pictures of how she wanted this book to look. Her mother, Bronwyne, brought it to life with illustrations. Callie is already coming up with more adventures for Glitter and Ellie.

Glitter the Unicorn
Lived in Pink
Cotton Candy Land.

Glitter the Unicorn
flew over the
Pink Cotton Candy
to her friend
Ellie's house.

Squishy gumdrops

were falling from the sky.

Glitter gave ELLie a ride to Cotton Candy Land, they were going on a treasure hunt.

Glitter and ELLie were Looking for the **Queen** of Cotton Candy Land.

The Queen of Cotton Candy Land gave them a metal map.

The
map
was
pink
and
purple.

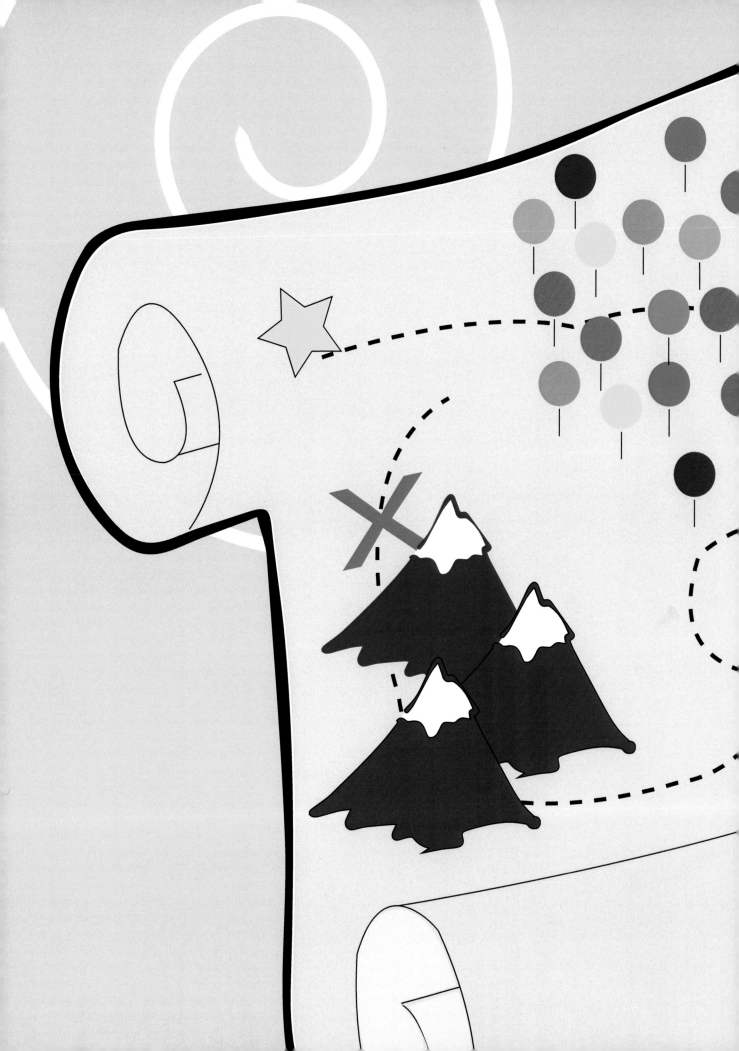

The map showed them
how they could go to
the **Lost Treasure**
of Candy.

Glitter and Ellie followed the map to the forest of Lollipops. Glitter and Ellie had fun eating the Lollipops.

Glitter found a clue
to go to the Mountain of Chocolate.

Glitter the Unicorn
gave Ellie a ride to the
Mountain of Chocolate.

On the tip top of the Mountain of Chocolate Glitter found the treasure.
It was a Chocolate Bar.

This Chocolate Bar
was the
Ultimate
Chocolate Bar.

It could make you **FLY.**

So Glitter the Unicorn gave
the Chocolate Bar to **ELLie.**

ELLie ate
the Chocolate Bar.

She Started to Fly.
Ellie was happy
she was flying
today of all days
on her birthday.

Glitter the Unicorn and Ellie
fly home together...

...down the
Mountain of Chocolate,
through
Lollipop Forest and
across
Pink Cotton Candy Land
to Ellie's house.

Then **ELLie** got to keep **GLitter** at her house.

Glitter was happy.
The End